Trevor and the Bon
Reading Book

Illustrated by Niall Harding
Written by Brenda Apsley

Thomas the Tank Engine & Friends

A BRITT ALLCROFT COMPANY PRODUCTION

Based on The Railway Series by The Rev W Awdry

© Gullane (Thomas) LLC 2003

Published in Great Britain in 2003 by Egmont Books Limited, 239 Kensington High Street, London, W8 6SA
Printed in China   ISBN 0 7498 5768 4

1 3 5 7 9 10 8 6 4 2

This pre-reading programme ...

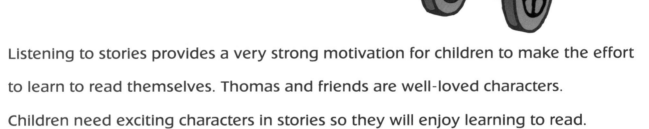

is designed to encourage an early confidence in reading.
It features the 45 frequent-use words as set out in the
National Curriculum, plus key vocabulary from the
Thomas Learning programme.

Listening to stories provides a very strong motivation for children to make the effort
to learn to read themselves. Thomas and friends are well-loved characters.
Children need exciting characters in stories so they will enjoy learning to read.

There is lots of repetition of key words and phrases. This encourages recognition of
words and the link between their sounds and shapes. Your child will also begin to
predict what is coming next, thus connecting written and spoken words, enabling
them to 'read'.

To get the most out of the Look and Say books:

· read the stories several times with your child on different occasions;

· read the speech in a lively, animated style and point to the words;

· encourage your child to read aloud the words he/she has learned.

Other activities to enjoy

· **Match the pictures**

Children will scan the page from left to right in preparation for reading and writing.

· **Find the pictures**

Children will learn to observe small details in this activity.

· **Spot the difference**

Children will compare two pictures - a skill used in reading when distinguishing letter shapes and words.

Thomas and Trevor were Really
Useful Engines.

One day, The Fat Controller went to
see them.

"We are going to make a bonfire,"
he said.

"I will bring the boys and girls,"
said Thomas.

"First we must make the fire,"
said The Fat Controller.

"Who can pull the logs of wood?"

"Not me," said Thomas.
"I can't pull logs."

"But I can!" said Trevor.
"I can pull logs."

"Who can saw the logs?"
said The Fat Controller.

"Not me," said Thomas.
"I can't saw logs."

"But I can!" said Trevor.
"I can saw logs."

Trevor worked hard, pulling and sawing logs.

The men worked hard, making a
big bonfire.

"You are Really Useful, Trevor,"
said The Fat Controller.

"Nearly as useful as me!" said Thomas.

Cheeky Thomas!

20 Draw a line between the pictures that are the same.

Point to these things in the picture.

Spot the difference!

Point to 5 differences between these two pictures.

Thomas Reading

(age 4-6)

Develop your child's reading confidence with these six reading books, companion activity books and flash cards.

Thomas Maths

(age 4-6)

Introduce your child to early maths skills with these six maths story books, companion activity books and flash cards.